Katie Morag
and the Wedding

For the Flautist

KATIE MORAG AND THE WEDDING
A RED FOX BOOK 978 1 782 95362 3

First published in Great Britain by The Bodley Head,
an imprint of Random House Children's Publishers UK
A Random House Group Company

The Bodley Head edition published 1995
Red Fox edition published 1997
Red Fox edition re-issued 2010
This Red Fox colour reader edition published 2014

3 5 7 9 10 8 6 4 2

Copyright © Mairi Hedderwick, 1995

Red Fox Books are published by Random House Children's Publishers UK,
61–63 Uxbridge Road, London W5 5SA

www.randomhousechildrens.co.uk
www.randomhouse.co.uk

Addresses for companies within The Random House Group Limited can be found at:
www.randomhouse.co.uk/offices.htm

THE RANDOM HOUSE GROUP Limited Reg. No. 954009

A CIP catalogue record for this book is available from the British Library.

Printed in China

Penguin Random House is committed to a sustainable future for our business, our readers and
our planet. This book is made from Forest Stewardship Council® certified paper.

MIX
Paper from
responsible sources
FSC® C018179

Katie Morag
and the Wedding

Mairi Hedderwick

RED FOX

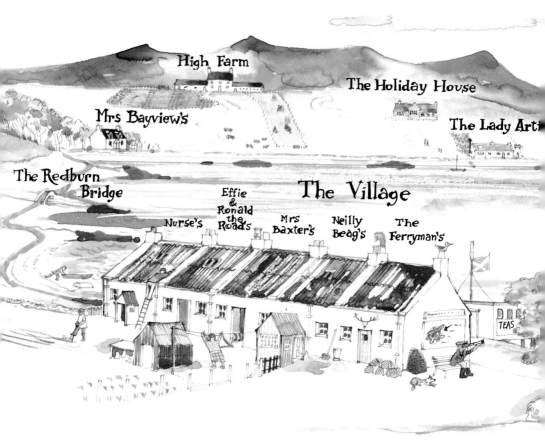

High Farm

The Holiday House

Mrs Bayview's

The Lady Art[ist]

The Redburn
Bridge

The Village

Effie
&
Ronald
the
Roads

Nurse's

Mrs
Baxter's

Neilly
Beag's

The
Ferryman's

TEAS

THE ISLE of STRUAY

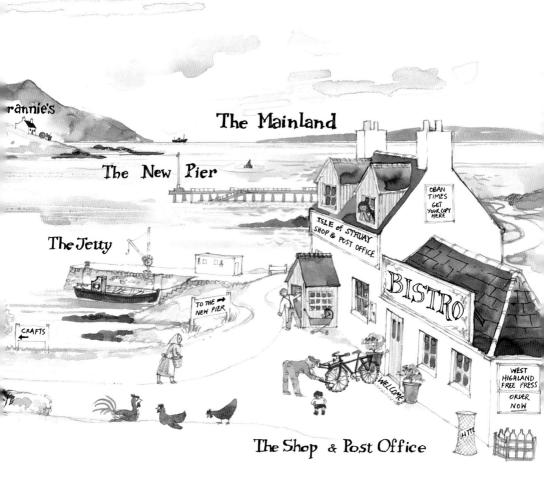

rannie's

The Mainland

The New Pier

The Jetty

ISLE of STRUAY
SHOP & POST OFFICE

OBAN
TIMES
GET
YOUR COPY
HERE

BISTRO

TO THE
NEW PIER

WEST
HIGHLAND
FREE PRESS

ORDER
NOW

CRAFTS

WELCOME

LITTER

The Shop & Post Office

Ever since the new pier had been built on the Isle of Struay, Granma Mainland visited regularly.

Katie Morag McColl was delighted to see more of her other grandmother. But most delighted of all the islanders was Neilly Beag. He fancied Granma Mainland and always looked so sad when she went away. Then he would write lots of long letters to her in the city on the Mainland and wait impatiently for the mailboat to bring back a reply.

This kept Mrs McColl, the Postmistress, very busy. Everyone on the island said a romance was afoot.

"Maybe even a wedding!" whispered the Ferryman's wife in between serving teas to the visitors.

"Pah! A wedding? I'll believe it
when I see it!" muttered Grannie
Island when she heard the gossip.
Katie Morag was very excited at
the thought of a wedding. It usually
meant a big party; it also meant that

the two people getting married
wanted to live together instead
of far apart.

Would Granma Mainland come
to live in Neilly Beag's house on the
island? That would be lovely! But,
oh dear, what if Neilly went to live
with Granma Mainland in the far
away city?

"If there is a wedding will Neilly
Beag be our grandad?" Katie Morag
asked when she and Liam arrived
at Grannie Island's, just in time
for dinner.

Her grannie did not answer.

"Wheesht! Go sit at the table!"
she frowned instead.

"We've got two grandmothers. Why don't we have two grandfathers?"

"Wheesht! Will you SIT DOWN!" glared Grannie Island.

It was a long time since Katie Morag had seen such a glower in Grannie Island's eye.

It was time to stop asking questions.

OLD PHOTOS

As Katie Morag pushed Liam homewards she wondered why Grannie Island was in such a bad mood. It made her feel sad.

When they got to the village Neilly Beag was at his front door.

He had a huge pile of stamped
addressed envelopes in his arms.

"The invitations for the wedding!"
he beamed proudly. "Can you
take them to the Post Office, Katie
Morag?"

That cheered Katie Morag up
no end.

"Can *we* go? Can *we* go?" chorused Katie Morag and Liam when the silver and gold invitation was put on the mantelpiece.

"Of course!" smiled Mr and Mrs McColl. "*Everyone* will be going to the wedding!"

"And the new baby?"

"Of course . . ."

"And the Ferryman and his wife . . . and the Lady Artist . . . and the new teacher?"

"Of course! Of course!" laughed

Mr and Mrs McColl.

"And Grannie Island?" asked Katie Morag.

Suddenly everything went very quiet in the McColl kitchen. Grown-ups can be very strange, thought Katie Morag, sometimes they answer questions and sometimes they do not . . .

That night in bed Katie Morag complained to Liam.

"If we didn't answer when we were asked questions we would be called rude."

"Rood!" agreed Liam.

"Granma Mainland always answers questions. I am going to write her a letter," declared Katie Morag.

This is what the letter said:

The next few weeks on the island were very busy.

All sorts of parcels and crates came off the boat and were carried up to Neilly's house or to the Village Hall.

Neilly dieted so much Mrs McColl had to get a needle and thread to alter his smart new suit. The Ferryman's wife made a giant of a chocolate cake; she and Mr McColl had to stand on stools to decorate it.

BULK ICING SUGAR

COCOA

Katie Morag and Liam made a special present for the bride and groom. The new baby lent ribbons for flags. Liam thought it was Christmas. He kept chanting "Anta Claws! Anta Claws!" and even hung up his stocking.

Katie Morag waited for a reply from Granma Mainland.

19

The day of the wedding drew near.

Granma Mainland and all the relatives and friends were due to arrive on the boat the day before the big event.

Nobody had seen Grannie Island for days.

All the islanders went to the pier to meet the guests arriving off the boat, but there was *no* sign of

Granma Mainland. Neilly Beag
was just about to burst into tears
when a loud clattering and whirring
reverberated around Village Bay.

It was a helicopter and Granma
Mainland was right in the front with
the white-bearded pilot.

"Anta Claws!" yelled Liam.

"It isn't Santa Claus, silly!" cried
Katie Morag. *She* knew who it was.

21

Grandad Island swung Katie Morag up in the air. "Last time I saw you, Katie Morag, you were just a sparkle in your mum and dad's eyes!"

Katie Morag and Liam raced Grandad Island up to the Village Hall to help with the decorations for the wedding party.

Grandad Island asked if Grannie Island was going to the wedding.

"You'd better go and find out for yourself," said Granma Mainland, somewhat sternly.

Katie Morag watched Grandad Island set off on the long walk round to Grannie Island's house, on the other side of the Bay. She worried that the fierce glare in Grannie Island's eye of late would frighten him away.

The Wedding Menu

LOBSTER CLAW SOUP
OR
STUFFED TURNIP
~
HAGGIS BURGERS
OR
CARROT STEAKS
~
CHIPS
~
CAKE & ICECREAM

Katie Morag need not have worried.

On the day of the wedding nobody's eyes were glaring – everyone's eyes were sparkling,

especially the two grandads'.
But Grannie Island's and Granma
Mainland's were the brightest
and sparkliest eyes of all.

Granma Mainland and Neilly
Beag were to honeymoon on the
neighbouring island of Fuay. There
were no people on Fuay, only sheep,
and they all belonged to Neilly.

"And all the lambs next spring
will be yours, Mrs Beag, my wee
Bobby Dazzler!"

Liam was right. Granma Mainland *was* going to have lots of babies to look after.

But Granma Mainland was not going to give up her flat in the city. She and Neilly would commute between Struay, Fuay and the Mainland. And Katie Morag could visit whenever she wanted.

It took a lot of persuading to get Grannie Island up in the helicopter. Grannie Island did not like travelling.

Grandad Island loved travelling and never stayed in one place for long.

"East, West, Home's Best!" insisted Grannie Island, clinging to her seat like a limpet.

Katie Morag knew then that Grandad Island would be leaving soon.

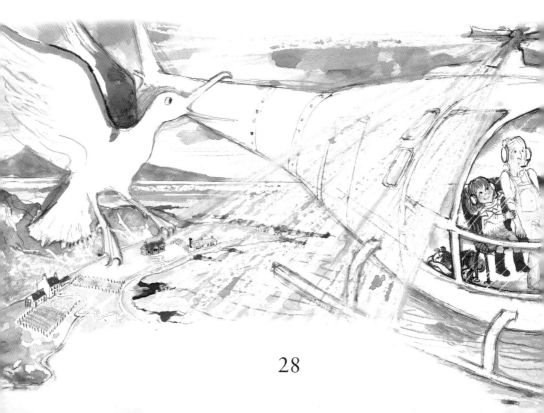

"Grandad, when you go travelling can I come too sometimes?"

"Certainly, Katie Morag – anywhere in the world."

Katie Morag was thrilled. She looked forward to visiting Fuay, the city on the Mainland and now, anywhere in the world!

But it was good to know that Grannie Island would always be there on the Island of Struay when she got back home.